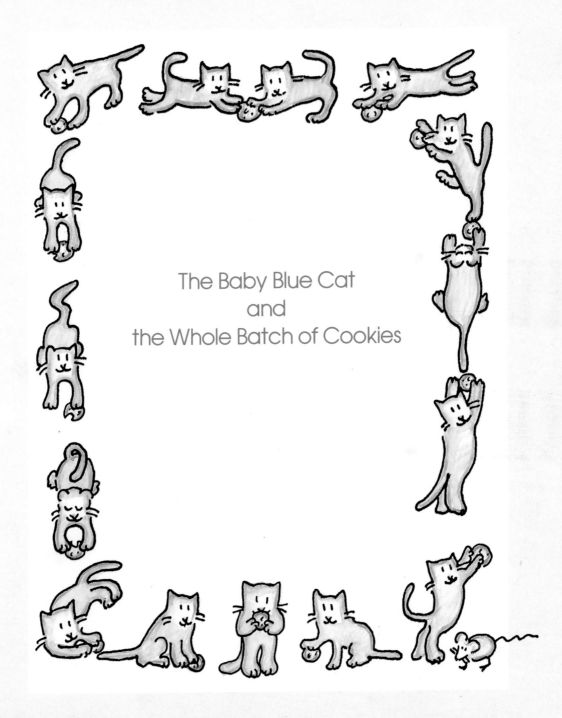

The Baby Blue Cat
and
the Whole Batch of Cookies

THE BABY BLUE CAT AND
THE WHOLE BATCH OF COOKIES

Ainslie Pryor

VIKING KESTREL

For my Grandparents
with special thanks

*Ainslie would like to gratefully acknowledge her
illustrious assistants, Lulu, Ricco and J.J.*

VIKING KESTREL
Published by the Penguin Group
Viking Penguin Inc., 40 West 23rd Street, New York, New York 10010, U.S.A.
Penguin Books Ltd, 27 Wrights Lane, London W8 5TZ, England
Penguin Books Australia Ltd, Ringwood, Victoria, Australia
Penguin Books Canada Ltd, 2801 John Street, Markham, Ontario, Canada L3R 1B4
Penguin Books (N.Z.) Ltd, 182–190 Wairau Road, Auckland 10, New Zealand

Penguin Books Ltd, Registered Offices: Harmondsworth, Middlesex, England

First published in 1989 by Viking Penguin Inc.

Published simultaneously in Canada

1 3 5 7 9 10 8 6 4 2

Library of Congress Cataloging in Publication Data
Pryor, Ainslie.   The baby blue cat and the whole batch of cookies
by Ainslie Pryor.   p.   cm.
Summary: When Mama Cat decides to make a special snack of milk and cookies,
Baby Blue Cat can't resist sneaking into the kitchen and eating the whole batch.
ISBN 0–670–81782–1 [1. Cats—Fiction] I. Title.   PZ7. P94964Bab 1989
[E]–dc 19   88–28760   CIP

Printed in Japan by Dai Nippon Printing Company, Inc.
Set in Avant Garde Book.

Have you heard the story
of the Baby Blue Cat and
the whole batch of cookies?

There was once a Mama Cat
and her four baby cats,

Baby Orange Cat, Baby White Cat,
Baby Striped Cat and Baby Blue Cat.

Mama Cat loved
all of her baby cats
very much.

The baby cats spent
most of their day playing
or helping Mama Cat
with her chores.

Sometimes Mama Cat
would fix her baby cats
a special treat.

Baby Orange Cat
especially liked cupcakes,
yum-yum.

 Baby White Cat
especially liked
strawberries and cream,
yum-yum.

Baby Striped Cat
especially liked
chocolate pudding,
in a glass, yum-yum.

Baby Blue Cat
was absolutely crazy
for raisins, yum-yum-yum!

But most of all, the baby cats
loved cookies.

One day Mama Cat baked
a whole batch of cookies
for her baby cats.

Mama Cat sat in her favorite chair.

"After play time," she said,
"we'll all have milk and cookies.
Would you like that?"
The Baby Cats all said, "Meow!"

While Mama Cat read her book
the baby cats went outside to play.

Except for Baby Blue Cat.
Baby Blue Cat was thinking,
thinking about cookies.

He wondered what kind of cookies
Mama Cat had baked.
He went to the kitchen
and there they were,
a whole plateful.

He picked *one* cookie up
and looked at it, very closely,
and before he knew it . . .

NIP NIP NIP

and the cookie was
gone gone gone
just like that.
It was an oatmeal cookie, yum-yum,
with raisins, wow meow!

Baby Blue Cat wondered if all
the cookies had raisins.

He took *two* cookies,
one in each paw and held them up
to see if they were the same,
and before he knew it . . .

NIP NIP NIP

and the two cookies were
gone gone
just like that.

Baby Blue Cat thought it would
be nice to take a cookie to each
of the other baby cats.

He hurried outside with the *three* cookies,
he stopped for just a moment
to see a bee, and before he knew it . . .

NIP NIP NIP

and the three cookies were
gone, all gone,
just like that.

Baby Blue Cat went back to the kitchen.
He was worried that it might look like
there were cookies missing.

No, there were plenty.
"One, two, three, four," he counted,
and before he knew it . . .

NIP NIP NIP

and the whole
batch of cookies was GONE,
just like that.

Baby Blue Cat looked
at the cookie plate.
There was not one cookie left.

"What will I do?" he asked,
"What will I do?"

Baby Blue Cat went to Mama Cat
and tugged at her apron.
He could hardly speak.

"M-M-Mama Cat, M-M-Mama Cat
I . . . I . . . I . . .," was all he could say.

Mama Cat picked up her Baby Blue Cat.
He had little cookie crumbs
all down his front.

"Did my Baby Blue Cat help himself
to a cookie or two?" she asked.

"Not one cookie, not two," he cried.
"THE WHOOOOOLE BATCH!"

Mama Cat gave her Baby Blue Cat
a hug. "My my my," she said.

Then Mama Cat called to Baby Orange Cat, Baby White Cat and Baby Striped Cat.

"I'm going to bake another batch of cookies," she said. "Then after nap time, we'll all have milk and cookies. Would you like that?"

"Meow," said Baby Orange Cat.
"Meow," said Baby White Cat.
"Meow," said Baby Striped Cat.

But Baby Blue Cat said "No."

And before he knew it . . .
with a slip slip slip

he was asleep sleep sleep
just like that.

And now you've heard the story
of the Baby Blue Cat and
the whole batch of cookies.